52 Crafts
for the
Christian Year

Collected from over 10 years of
the respected Christian education
curriculum and worship resource
The Whole People of God, these
volumes offer tried and true
material in easy-to-use format.
These are proven resources with
a theology and approach that
thousands have come to trust.

52 Crafts

FOR THE CHRISTIAN YEAR

Compiled by Donna Scorer

Illustrated by Crystal Przybille

WOOD LAKE BOOKS

Editor: Cheryl Perry
Cover design: Margaret Kyle
Interior design: Julie Bachewich
Consulting art director: Robert MacDonald
Cover photo: Dan Mawson, Photographic Resources

At Wood Lake Books, we practice what we publish, guided by a concern for fairness, justice,
and equal opportunity in all of our relationships with employees and customers.

We acknowledge the financial support of the Government of Canada through the
Book Publishing Industry Development Program for our publishing activities.

Canadian Cataloguing in Publication Data
Scorer, Donna, 1944–
52 crafts for the Christian year
Includes index.
ISBN 1-55145-295-2
1. Bible crafts. 2. Handicraft. I. Przybille, Crystal. II. Perry,
Cheryl, 1970– III. Title. IV. Title: Fifty-two crafts for the Christian year.
BS613.S36 1998   754.5'088'204   C98-910151-7

Printing 10 9 8 7 6 5 4 3 2

Published by Wood Lake Books
Kelowna, British Columbia, Canada

Printed in Canada by
Cariboo Press, Vernon, British Columbia

Contents

As You Begin...

The crafts presented in this book are offered for all those who have the joyful privilege of helping children learn about God and God's love for us.

We have grouped the ideas into sections according to the seasons of the Christian year. Many denominations organize their worship and church life following the calendar of the Church Year and the lectionary. With this book organized in the same way, we hope you will find it easy to plan activities for home or church that reflect these themes.

Key scripture verses accompany each craft. Several translations, and paraphrases, have been used for these verses. Many crafts can be adapted for other Bible stories, themes or church seasons. We have included some suggestions. (Also see cross-referenced Index at the back of this book.)

Get to know your children before beginning; there is a wide range of abilities within a group of young children. Some children may not yet have mastered scissor skills. Some activities need more adult involvement than others. Always supervise while allowing children to grow in their independence and creativity.

If you are planning to use these crafts with a child at home:

- Choose crafts that are appropriate for the skills of the child but do not dismiss more difficult crafts. Work with the child, helping with tasks they can't handle alone.
- If a particular craft material is not available, substitute! Often it becomes an improvement over the original plan.

If you are planning to use these crafts with a group of children at church:

- Gather materials needed in advance.
- Make a sample of the craft to be sure the directions are fully understood.
- When working with very young children you may need to prepare part of the craft ahead of time.
- Feel free to adapt the crafts or vary the materials required.

It is possible to purchase crayons, construction paper, pencils, felt markers, and tempera paint that enable children to creatively reflect the multi-ethnic nature of the society in which we live. Encourage their use.

What are the Seasons of the Church Year?

Season of Advent

The Season of Advent begins four weeks before Christmas and marks the beginning of the Church Year. The dates change from year to year – the first Sunday in Advent falls on the Sunday nearest November 30. Depending on which day Christmas Eve falls, the season can last from 22 to 28 days. The word *advent* means "coming." It is a season of preparation, expectation and hope. During the Advent Season we prepare for the birth of Christ, and the renewal of our faith, and we look to the future and the coming of God's reign.

Christmas

The joyous Season of Christmas begins on December 25 (or at sundown on December 24) when we hear about the angels telling the Good News to shepherds outside Bethlehem. The season lasts 12 days, ending with the Feast of Epiphany on January 6, when we celebrate the visit of the Magi from the East.

Season after Epiphany (Ordinary Time)

January 6, the Feast of Epiphany, marks the end of the Christmas Season, and the beginning of a time known as the Sundays after Epiphany. Some call this period "Ordinary Time" while others refer to it as the Season after Epiphany. The word *epiphany* means "showing forth." During this season, we see God's glory and purpose as shown through the life of Jesus and his followers. This season focuses on God's light spreading through the teaching and healing ministry of Jesus.

Season of Lent

Lent officially begins with Ash Wednesday and continues until Easter Day. It is a time to pay special attention to the work of God in our lives, our community and the world in which we live. It is a time of preparation, reflection, growth, and change – a time to take stock, both of ourselves and our society. The season lasts 40 days (not including Sundays) to symbolize the 40 days Jesus spent in the wilderness preparing for his public ministry. Our English word *lent* comes from the word "lengthen." In the Northern Hemisphere, Lent takes place as the days lengthen into Spring.

Season of Easter

Easter is the focal point of the Christian Year. It is a time to celebrate Christ's resurrection and the birth of the early church by reading the Easter stories from the gospels and remembering stories of how the early church started. The Easter Season culminates in Pentecost, the festival of fire, wind and the Holy Spirit. We recall that the Holy Spirit was poured out on the disciples. We celebrate the gifts of the Spirit each of us has been given, and we celebrate that God's Spirit continues to be present among us.

Season after Pentecost

This is the season of the Church Year when we celebrate the growth of the church after Pentecost and explore what it means for us to live faithfully in the world today. This season places particular emphasis on social justice that calls us to reach beyond ourselves to the poor, the marginalized, and the outsider.

Advent Calendar Poster

Advent is a time of waiting and preparing for the celebration of Jesus' birth. The word Advent means "coming."

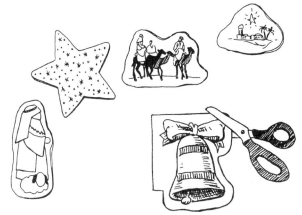

Materials Needed

- old Christmas cards
- large piece of green poster board
- a star shape pattern (see p. 62)
- aluminum foil or yellow construction paper
- pencil
- scissors
- glue stick

With the Child

1. Look through old Christmas cards and cut out 24 small pictures for tree ornaments.
2. Use the star pattern to cut out a star from aluminum foil or construction paper.
3. On a sheet of green poster board draw the outline of a Christmas tree. Make sure it is large enough to accommodate the 24 ornaments that will be added.
4. Pencil in a numbered dot for each day of Advent on the tree. Then add a dot for December 25, Christmas Day, at the top. *(See illustration.)*
5. Place this Advent calendar poster in an accessible location such as on the refrigerator door or classroom wall.
6. Place the ornaments in an envelope or basket. Each day glue one ornament on top of the dot for that day.
7. On Christmas Day a star could be added to the top of the tree.

For God so loved the world that God gave God's only child, so that everyone who believes in that Child may not perish but may have eternal life.   *(John 3:16)*

Advent Wreath

The Advent wreath is a circle that goes round and round, and reminds us of God's love that has no end.

Materials Needed
- play dough (for recipe see p. 61)
- 3 drinking straws
- a plastic lid
- yellow construction paper
- an envelope
- scissors

With the Child
1. Make green play dough.
2. Cut straws in half to create candles. Cut a slit in the top of each.
3. Cut five flame shapes from construction paper.
4. Put some green play dough on the lid.
5. Stick four straws into the play dough around the edge of the lid. Place the fifth straw in the middle.
6. Place paper flames in an envelope.
7. Each Sunday during Advent add a flame (i.e. place in slits cut in the straws). On Christmas Day add the last flame to the candle in the center.

Options
- Stick tiny pinecones, dried berries or evergreen needles into the play dough.
- Use purple or blue straws and one white straw for the middle.

Those who walked in the dark have seen a bright light. And it shines upon everyone who lives in the land of darkest shadows. (Isaiah 9:2)

Megaphone

Practice making Advent announcements through this megaphone. "Hear ye! Hear ye! The Messiah is coming!"

Materials Needed

- a clean plastic bottle with a handle
- permanent felt markers
- crepe paper streamers
- self-adhesive stickers
- scissors or serrated knife

With the Child

1. Cut off the bottom of the plastic bottle.
2. Decorate the bottle with stickers and felt markers.
3. Tie several crepe paper streamers to the handle of the bottle.
4. Practice making Advent announcements.

Other Connections

- Call of the Disciples
- The Call of Samuel

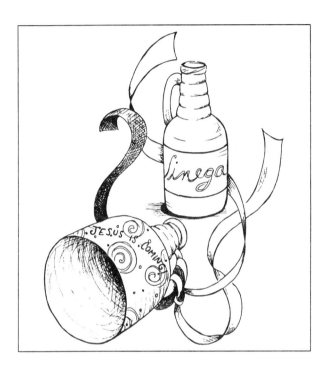

Jerusalem, go up on a high mountain and proclaim the good news!
(Isaiah 40:9)

Paper Plate Angel

This angel sits well on a flat surface or over the top spike of a Christmas tree.

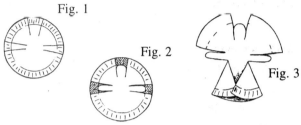

Fig. 1

Fig. 2

Fig. 3

Materials Needed

- thin (bendable) paper plate or tinfoil pie plate
- scissors
- felt markers or crayons
- lace doilies (optional)
- stapler or tape

With the Child

1. Draw the cutting lines on the paper plate (Fig. 1).
2. Cut along the marked lines and round off arms and head (Fig. 2).
3. Decorate with felt markers or crayons. Glue lace doily pieces to the wings.
4. Fold skirt back and tape or staple (Fig. 3).
5. If using a tinfoil pie plate, flatten the crimped edges to form wings. Bend wings back and head forward slightly.

Other Connections

- The Annunciation
- Joseph's Dream
- Easter – use to tell the story of Jesus' resurrection

An angel of the Lord appeared to them, and the glory of the Lord shone over them. The shepherds were terribly afraid.   *(Luke 2:9)*

Scented Card

We can be God's messengers too. We can tell others the Good News about baby Jesus.

Materials Needed
- construction paper
- a Christmas pattern such as bell, star, angel, manger (see p. 63)
- sandpaper
- scissors
- fine-line felt markers
- cinnamon stick

With the Child
1. Fold a piece of construction paper to create a card.
2. Use the Christmas symbol pattern to cut a shape out of sandpaper.
3. Glue the shape to the front of the card.
4. Print a message on the outside and a Good News message or scripture verse on the inside.
5. Rub a cinnamon stick over the sandpaper to release a cinnamon smell.

Other Connections
- Celebration – change the shape and use for a birthday card or other festive occasion.

This very day in King David's hometown a Savior is born for you. He is Christ the Lord.   *(Luke 2:11)*

Life-size Message

Send this life-size person to someone the child won't be able to share the Christmas Season with.

Fig. 1

Materials Needed
- mural paper or a large sheet of newsprint
- tempera paint or felt markers
- ribbon
- mailing tube

With the Child
1. Have child lie down on the mural paper and trace the outline of their body.
2. Paint or color in facial features and clothing.
3. Have the child print a message to someone they can't wait to see at Christmas or for someone who will not be able to share Christmas with them.
4. Roll up the paper figure and tie with ribbon.
5. Put the life-size message in a large envelope or tube and mail it to the chosen person.

Other Connections
- Outreach – send this life-size message instead of a card to someone who is ill, needs cheering up, has a birthday.
- Celebrations – send to a grandparent to show physical growth.

Look, I am going to send a messenger to prepare a way before me.
(Malachi 3:1a)

Stained Glass Window

This is a very easy way to make a simple stained glass window without a mess – no glue involved!

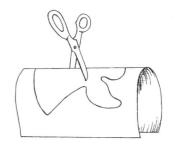

Materials Needed

- construction paper
- a Christmas shape pattern (see p. 63)
- clear adhesive covering (e.g. MacTac, Con-Tact)
- variety of multicolored items (e.g. tissue paper, yarn scraps, sequins, confetti)
- scissors

With the Child

1. Use the Christmas pattern to cut a shape out of the center of the construction paper. (Trace pattern in center, fold sheet slightly and snip with scissors. Insert scissors in slit and cut away inner part of shape.)
2. Place a piece of clear adhesive covering, with backing removed, over the opening and press.
3. Turn the construction paper over so that the sticky side faces up.
4. Press small multicolored items on the shape. (The sticky surface eliminates the need for glue.)
5. Then lay a single sheet of tissue paper over the adhesive covering.
6. Tape this picture to a window so the light shines through it.

Other Connections

- Epiphany – use a star or crown.
- Easter – cut out a cross shape and press on tiny flower petals.
- Pentecost – use a dove shape or flames.

On you the light of the Lord will shine; the brightness of God's presence will be with you.   *(Isaiah 60:2b, c)*

Framed Picture

Baby Jesus is God's special gift of love to us. We celebrate by giving gifts to others.

Materials Needed

- a metal preserving jar ring
- 2 white paper circles cut to fit inside the ring
- felt markers or crayons
- clear adhesive covering (e.g. MacTac, Con-Tact)
- clear tape
- ribbon
- yarn

With the Child

1. Draw pictures on the two white paper circles.
2. Cover with clear adhesive covering.
3. Place the pictures back to back and tape inside the metal ring.
4. Wrap colorful ribbon around the outside of the ring and make a bow.
5. Add a yarn loop for hanging.

Option

- Place only one drawing inside the ring and substitute a bright colored paper circle for the other drawing.
- Use regular jar lids and glue pictures on both sides.
- Substitute old Christmas cards for drawings.
- Substitute child's picture for drawings.

Other Connections

- Project – make a Bible story tree by placing a large branch in a bucket of stones. After reading each Bible story draw a scene from it and hang it on the story tree.

Remember that our Lord Jesus said, "More blessings come from giving than from receiving."   *(Acts 20:35b)*

Tanabata Decoration

This is a popular decoration in Japan.

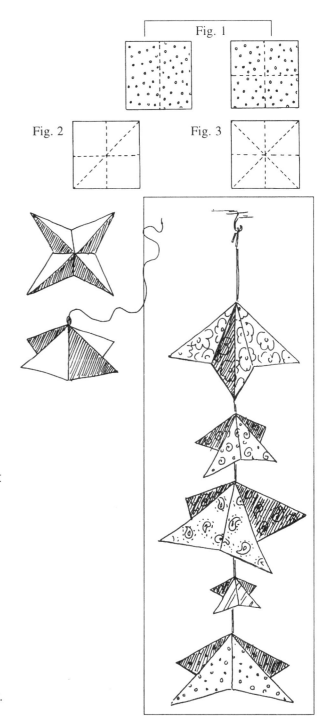

Fig. 1

Fig. 2 Fig. 3

Materials Needed
- colored paper (e.g. origami paper or lightweight paper)
- felt markers
- pencils
- string and needle
- scissors

With the Child
1. Cut paper into different sized squares.
2. Fold each square in half and then fold it in half again (Fig. 1).
3. Unfold the square. Turn it over and fold it on the diagonal (Fig. 2).
4. Unfold it and fold on the other diagonal (Fig. 3).
5. Push the paper gently together and up to form a pyramid. Make several pyramids.
6. Thread a needle with string. Tie a knot at the end.
7. Insert needle through center of pyramid and push it through the top of the pyramid. Thread several pyramids onto each string. (Optional: Tie a knot between each pyramid.)
8. Hang on the Christmas tree or from the ceiling.

Options
- On the inside of each pyramid, print the name of a person to be remembered during this season.

Other Connections
- Pentecost – make orange, yellow, and red pyramids. Hang it in an area where a breeze will move it.

Thanks be to God for God's indescribable gift!   *(2 Corinthians 9:15)*

God's Eye

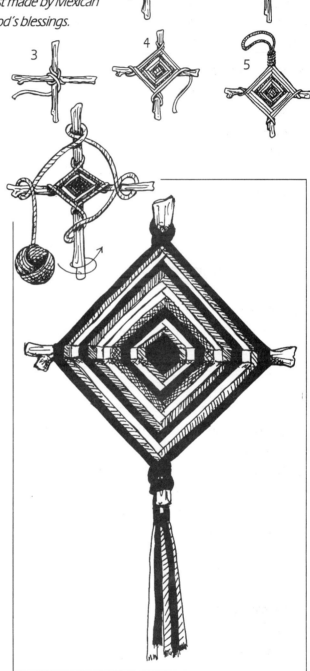

Ojo de Dios *means "eye of God" in Spanish. These were first made by Mexican Indians to hang in their homes as a constant reminder of God's blessings.*

Materials Needed
- 2 sticks (e.g. chopsticks, twigs, Popsicle sticks)
- a variety of colored yarn

With the Child
1. Cross the 2 sticks and tie an end of yarn around them where they cross.
2. Weave the yarn over one stick, then around and under, then over the stick toward the next stick. *(See illustration.)*
3. Continue around the square doing the same thing for all the rows.
4. Change colors by tying the new color to one of the sticks and continuing the weaving pattern.
5. When finished, hang it on the Christmas tree.

Option
- Tie a small tassel to the end of each stick. To make tassel: Wind yarn around three fingers many times. (Note: Not too tight.) Remove from the fingers and tie one end with a piece of yarn. Cut the other end to form the tassel. *(See illustration.)*

Other Connections
- Pentecost – use orange, yellow, and red yarn. Make as a reminder that the Spirit of God is with us. Hang outside where a breeze will make it move.

May your constant love be with us, God, as we put our hope in you.
(Psalm 33:22)

A Little Manger

This manger might be made at the beginning of the Advent Season. Then, each day a little straw could be added to the manger. Baby Jesus is placed in the manger on Christmas Day.

Materials Needed

- construction paper
- scissors
- toilet paper roll
- glue
- straw, dried grass, or torn pieces of yellow tissue paper or construction paper
- peanut (in the shell)
- small self-adhesive sticker or scrap of construction paper
- small piece of cloth or facial tissue

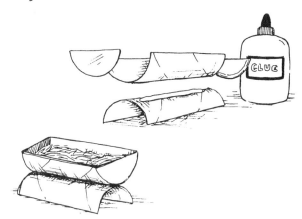

With the Child

1. On construction paper, trace a circle using the end of the toilet roll as a pattern.
2. Cut the circle in half.
3. Cut the toilet paper tube in half lengthwise. Separate and glue back-to-back.
4. Glue a half circle on ends of the tube to create the manger.
5. Fill manger with straw (dried grass, or torn pieces of yellow tissue or construction paper).
6. For baby Jesus – Use an unshelled peanut and glue on a small oval piece of paper (or sticker) for a face. Draw eyes and nose. Wrap in facial tissue or scrap of cloth.

Other Connections

- Moses – use the top half of the manger as a reed basket for baby Moses.

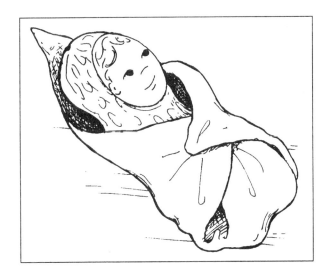

You will find a baby wrapped in cloths and lying in a manger.

(Luke 2:12b)

Epiphany Star Streamers

The scriptures tell us a star led the Magi to the place where Jesus was. March around the room or through the church with this star carried high up in the air.

Materials Needed

- poster board
- star pattern (see p. 63)
- scissors
- a dowel
- long tinsel or crepe paper streamers
- tape
- stapler
- glue stick and glitter (optional)

With the Child

1. Using the pattern, cut two stars from poster board.
2. Tape streamers and dowel to one poster board star.
3. Tape or staple both stars together.
   (See illustration.)
4. Optional: Using a glue stick, glue glitter onto both sides of the star.

Other Connections

- Baptism – use a dove shape and blue steamers.
- Noah's Ark – use a rainbow shape and suspend a variety of colored streamers from each end.
- Easter – use a cross covered in flowers and a variety of colored streamers suspended from it.

Arise, shine, your light has come.   *(Isaiah 60:1a)*

Baptismal Candle Card

Make a welcome card for a baby who will be baptized. This card could be presented to the parents of the baby.

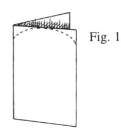

Fig. 1

Materials Needed
- white and yellow construction paper
- scissors
- felt markers or crayons
- glitter or gummed stars
- glue stick

With the Child
1. Fold white construction paper in half and round off the top with scissors (Fig. 1).
2. Cut an oval section from the front of the card (Fig. 2).
3. Cut out and glue a yellow flame onto the top (i.e. inside of card).
4. Decorate the card front with glitter or gummed stars, felt markers or crayons.
5. Print a message on the inside of the card (e.g. "You are my Beloved Child").

Other Connections
- Easter – make an Easter (Paschal) candle and print an Easter message inside.

Fig. 2

cut out

you are my Beloved Child

You are my beloved child. I am pleased with you.   *(Luke 3:22b)*

Dove

When Jesus was baptized the dove was a reminder to him that God's Spirit was with him. God's Spirit is with us, too.

Materials Needed

- construction paper
- a dove shape pattern (see p. 62)
- toilet paper tube or paper towel tube
- felt markers or crayons
- scissors

With the Child

1. Using the dove pattern, cut out a construction paper dove.
2. Decorate the dove and the tube with felt markers or crayons.
3. Make two short slits opposite one another on one end of the tube.
4. Gently slide the tail of the paper dove into the slit. Tape side extensions down to keep it in place.
5. Gently move the tube up and down and the dove's wings will flap as if flying.

Other Connections

- Noah's Ark
- Pentecost – the dove is a symbol of the Holy Spirit.

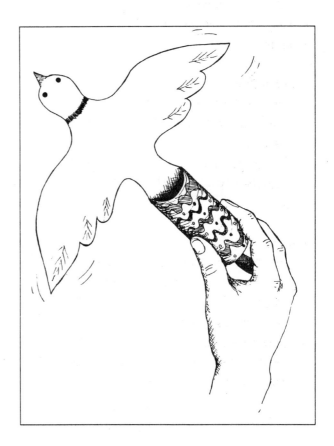

As he prayed, the sky opened up, and the Holy Spirit came down upon him in the form of a dove. 					(Luke 3:21b-22)

Name in Lights

This is a reminder that God's light shines in us.

Materials Needed
- a disposable meat tray
- ballpoint pen or marker
- large nail

With the Child
1. Turn the disposable tray over so that there is a raised surface. Print child's name in big letters on the surface.
2. With a large nail, poke holes into the letters.
3. Hold the tray up to the light to see the name light up.

Options
- Print "God Calls" in small letters on the top of the tray. Print name in large letters underneath it. When you hold the tray up to the light, say "God calls...*[child's name]*."
- Draw a heart and print "*[child's name]* Loves Jesus." Poke holes in the name and around the heart shape.

God has made light shine in our hearts, to bring us the knowledge of God's glory shining in the face of Christ. (2 Corinthians 4:6b)

Twirling Fish Mobile

Jesus calls all of us to be his helpers.

Materials Needed

- strips of white poster board
- a wire clothes hanger or paper plate
- felt markers or crayons
- needle or tape and thread or yarn
- scissors

With the Child

1. Lay the poster board strip lengthwise on a flat surface.
2. Approx. 1 in. (2.5cm) from the top of the strip, cut a slit from right to left. Be careful not to cut all the way through the strip (Fig. 1).
3. Approx. 1 in. (2.5cm) from the bottom of the strip, cut a slit from left to right. Be careful not to cut all the way through (Fig. 2).
4. Color one side of the strip with bright colors and on the other side print a way to answer Jesus' call to follow him.
5. To construct fish, fold or bend each strip and fit one slit into the other.
6. Sew or tape thread or yarn to the top of each fish. Suspend from a paper plate or hanger.

Other Connections

- Call of the Disciples
- Feeding of the Five Thousand – add bread shapes as well.

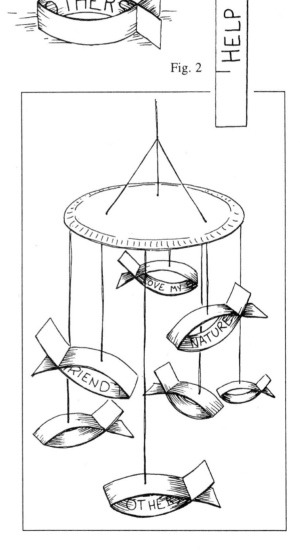

Fig. 1

Fig. 2

HELP OTHERS

Jesus said, "Come with me and I will teach you to be fishers of people."
(Mark 1:17)

Paper Plate Fish

*In the Season after Epiphany we hear the story of Jesus calling his first
disciples, who were fishers.*

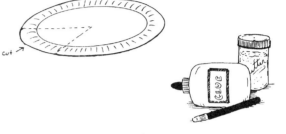

Materials Needed

- a paper plate
- scissors
- stapler
- felt markers or crayons
- decorative materials (e.g. glitter, cellophane, scraps
  of construction paper, etc.)

With the Children

1. Mark a triangle on a paper plate and cut it out.
   (See illustration.)
2. Staple the triangle to the plate to form the tail.
3. Decorate the fish with felt markers, glitter, cellophane pieces, construction paper shapes, etc.

Other Connections

- Jonah
- Feeding of the Five Thousand
- Call of the Disciples
- Early Christians – the fish was a sign used by the
  early Christians.

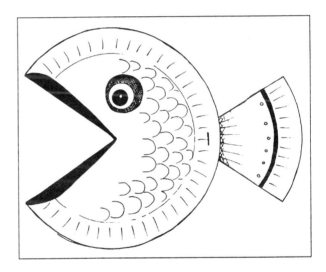

They pulled the boats up on the beach, left everything, and followed Jesus.
(Luke 5:11)

Jesus' Shoes

What would it be like to walk in Jesus' shoes?

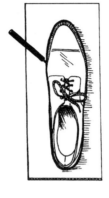

Materials Needed

- cardboard
- a pair of adult shoes
- scissors
- felt markers or crayons
- thick rubber bands

With the Child

1. Trace a pair of adult shoes on cardboard and cut them out.
2. (Optional: Decorate with felt markers or crayons.)
3. Attach to the bottom of the child's shoes with rubber bands. (Place rubber bands over the bridge of the child's foot.)
4. Take a few moments to think what it would have been like to travel with Jesus and his disciples. Then take a walk in the cardboard shoes.

Other Connections

- Call of the Disciples
- Biblical Clothing – make these sandals to dress up and play-act life in Bible times.
- Lent – use these to enhance a walk through the events of Holy Week with children.
- Early Christians – use these shoes to talk about the travels of the apostles who spread the good news about Jesus.

Jesus went all over Galilee, teaching in the synagogues, preaching the Good News about the kingdom, and healing people.　　*(Matthew 4:23)*

Camera

Make a camera, go for a walk, and take pictures of all the wondrous things God has created in our world.

Materials Needed

- a small box (e.g. gelatin box, soup box, individual cereal boxes)
- white paper
- a thin piece of colored plastic or a cardboard slide frame
- a tiny piece of sponge
- paper egg carton
- white glue
- tape
- yarn
- scissors
- felt markers or crayons

With the Child

1. Cover a small box with the white paper.
2. Tape an empty slide frame or piece of colored plastic on the back for a viewer. *(See illustration.)*
3. Glue a small piece of soft sponge for a shutter release.
4. Glue one section from an egg carton for the lens.
5. When glue is dry, color the camera with felt markers or crayons.
6. Tape yarn to the sides of the camera so that it can hang around the neck.

Other Connections

- Creation Story
- Spring
- Christian Family Sunday: take pictures of God's family.

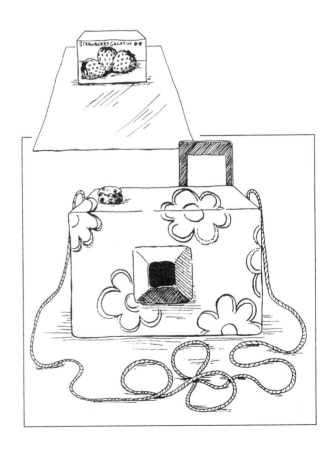

Praise the Lord, my soul! O Lord, my God, how great you are!

(Psalm 104:1a)

Feelings Stick

God loves us no matter how we feel. As a reminder, put this stick in a special place – a pocket, a book, in a cup, by the bed.

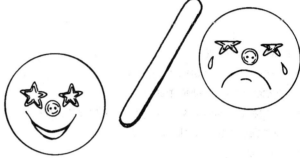

Materials Needed
- construction paper
- scissors
- felt markers, decorative materials (e.g. glitter, small stickers, stars)
- masking tape
- Popsicle stick
- white glue

With the Child
1. Cut two 3 in. (7.5 cm) circles of colored construction paper.
2. Using decorative materials, make a happy face on one circle and a different feeling face (e.g. angry, sad, worried, afraid) on the other circle.
3. Tape one end of the Popsicle stick to the back of a paper face. Glue the back of the other circle over the taped stick (i.e. the circles are glued back-to-back).
4. A message could be printed on the Popsicle stick using a fine-line marker.

Other Connections
- Jesus and the Children – draw an upset face on one side to show how the disciples felt and a happy face on the other to show how the children felt when Jesus welcomed them.
- Bible Verses – print a favorite verse on the stick.

O God, I know that your love will last for all time.   *(Psalm 89:2a)*

"God's Love" Mobile

God's love includes all people.

Materials Needed

- large sheet of construction paper
- pencil and fine-line markers
- magazine pictures of people of different ages, gender, ethnic backgrounds
- scissors
- a hole punch
- yarn
- a wire clothes hanger

With the Child

1. Draw an arc shape on a large piece of construction paper. *(See illustration.)*
2. Trace a hand at each end of the arc. Cut out.
3. Decorate the arc and print a message to go around it (e.g. "God's love includes all people").
4. Cut circles from construction paper.
5. Cut out a variety of people's faces from magazines and mount on construction paper circles.
6. Punch a small hole in each circle. Thread yarn through holes.
7. Tie the faces at different levels onto the bottom edge of a hanger.
8. Tape the "hug" shape to the hanger.
   (See illustration.)

Other Connections

- Project – make a "Class Tree of Love." Use pictures children have drawn or photographs of the children in your class.

God is not far from any of us...In God we live, and move, and exist...We too are God's children.　*(Acts 17:27b, 28a)*

Mystery Picture

In the Transfiguration story, the disciples saw Jesus in a new way and felt the awesome mystery of God.

Materials Needed
- white construction paper
- sheet of red (not pink) cellophane (same size as construction paper)
- felt markers or crayons
- stapler

With the Child
1. Color a picture on construction paper with all the colors of markers (including yellow and orange).
2. Staple a piece of red cellophane to the top edge of the picture.
3. Watch some of the lines disappear and reappear as the cellophane is laid down and lifted up.

Other Connections
- Parable of the Lost Sheep – draw a scene using all the colors except yellow and orange. Draw the lost sheep with either yellow or orange. When the red cellophane is laid over the picture the sheep can't be seen. Lift it up to find the lost sheep!

All of us...are being transformed into God's likeness in an ever greater degree of glory.   *(2 Corinthians 3:18b)*

Desert Footprint

Lent is the beginning of a journey with Jesus.

Materials Needed

- construction paper
- scissors
- masking tape
- white glue
- glue spreaders or small brushes
- dry sand

With the child

1. Trace child's foot (with or without shoe on) on a piece of construction paper.
2. Cut out the footprint.
3. Attach a small piece of masking tape to the underside of the footprint and tape it to a larger piece of construction paper.
4. Using a glue spreader or small brush, spread white glue around the edges of the footprint. (Note: It is easier to start each brush stroke from the inside of the footprint, across the edge and onto the background paper.)
5. Sprinkle sand over the glue.
6. Carefully remove the footprint and there remains a footprint in the sand!

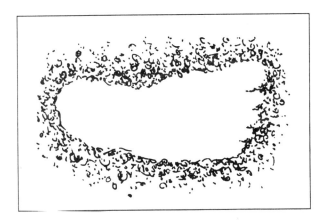

Other Connections

- Abraham and Sarah
- Moses
- John the Baptist

The Spirit led Jesus into the desert to be tested.   *(Matthew 4:1)*

Lenten Chain

The Season of Lent lasts 40 days (plus 6 Sundays) to remind us of the time Jesus spent in the wilderness. This is a chain used to mark off the days from Ash Wednesday to Easter Sunday.

Materials Needed

- purple, white and another color of construction paper
- scissors
- stapler or clear tape

With the Child

1. Cut strips of construction paper approx. 1 x 6 in. (2.5 x 15cm). You will need 40 purple strips, 1 white strip, and 6 strips of another color.
2. Create a chain by stapling or taping the first strip into a circle. Put the second strip through the first circle and staple or tape. Continue with all the strips until a long chain is formed. The order will be: purple chains for weekdays, color of your choice for the 6 Sundays, and 1 white link representing Easter Sunday. (Note: Remember Lent begins on a Wednesday!)
3. Hang the chain in a special place and remove one link each day to count the days of Lent.

Other Connections

- Advent – use light purple or blue construction paper for strips in the Advent chain. The last link would be removed on Christmas Day.

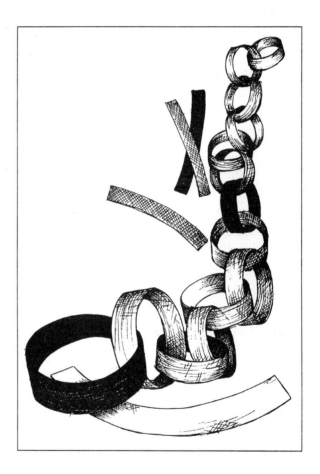

Get the road ready for the Lord; make a straight path for him to travel!

(Luke 3:4c)

Butterfly Calendar

The 6 Sundays that fall during Lent are not included in the 40 days because every Sunday is "a little Easter" – a celebration of Jesus' resurrection. Here is another way to mark off the days until we celebrate Easter Day.

Materials Needed

- a large butterfly pattern (see p. 64)
- construction paper
- scissors
- 46 colored cotton balls (see instructions p. 61)
- church or Bible stickers (optional)
- crayons or felt markers
- a large envelope
- glue stick

With the Child

1. Using the butterfly pattern, cut a butterfly out of construction paper.
2. Print the numbers 1– 40 on the butterfly and draw a small church or Bible to indicate each Sunday. (Optional: Use a church or Bible sticker.)
3. Color the butterfly (except the head).
4. Put 46 colored cotton balls inside an envelope.
5. On Ash Wednesday, glue the first cotton ball on the number 1. *(See illustration.)*
6. Add one cotton ball each day through Lent.
7. Each day check the calendar to see how much of the butterfly has been filled in and how close we are to Easter.
8. On Easter Sunday, color the head of the butterfly.

Other Connections

Eliminate the numbers and drawings and simply glue the colored cotton balls onto the construction paper to create a beautiful butterfly. Use this idea for:

- Easter
- Spring

This is the day made memorable by God; what immense joy for us!

(Psalm 118:24)

Pretzels

A long time ago, people held their arms crossed over their chests when they prayed. Pretzels were first made to remind people to pray.

Materials Needed
- pretzel recipe and ingredients (for recipe see p. 61)
- cookie sheet

With the Child
1. Prepare the dough.
2. For each pretzel use a piece of dough the size of a walnut.
3. Roll into a long "snake." Bend two ends around and cross over. Pinch dough together where it touches.
4. Sprinkle with coarse salt.
5. Bake at 400 degrees F (200 degrees C) for about 15 minutes. This depends on size. Less time is needed if pretzels are small and thin, more if they are larger and thicker.

Options
- An older child might think of what they would like to pray for; print each prayer on a small square of paper, and attach each one to a pretzel.
- Give the pretzels to others with a prayer reminder or a request for a prayer.

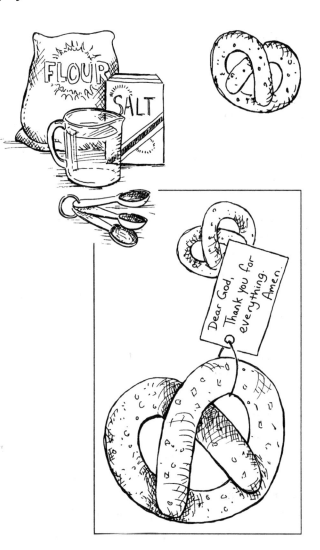

Do all this in prayer, asking for God's help. (Ephesians 6:18a)

Prayer Pocket

One way to talk to God is through pictures.

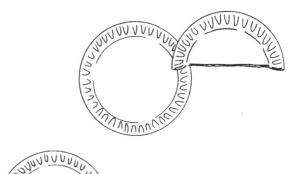

Materials Needed

- 2 paper plates
- scissors
- stapler
- crayons or felt markers
- hole punch
- yarn
- tape

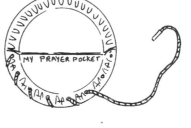

With the Child

1. Cut one paper plate in half.
2. Staple a half plate to the bottom of a whole plate.
3. Print "My Prayer Pocket" along the edge.
4. Punch holes all around the stapled edge.
5. Tie approx. 20 in. (50cm) piece of yarn to one end of the pocket.
6. Wrap a small piece of tape around the other end of the yarn to form a "needle."
7. Use the needle to lace plates together.
8. Decorate the plate with crayons or markers.
9. Fill the Prayer Pocket with pictures of what the child would like to say to God.

Other Connections

- Advent – fill the pocket with 24 small figures cut from old Christmas cards. Include a picture of baby Jesus. Each day pull out one figure. On Christmas day take out the last figure, baby Jesus.
- Advent – add yellow "love" strips each day to fill the pocket (i.e. manger). Add a play dough baby Jesus on Christmas Day (see recipe on p. 61).

May my words and my thoughts be acceptable to you, O God, my strength and my deliverer.   *(Psalm 19:14)*

Wheel Painting

Wherever we go, God is always with us.

Materials Needed
- small toy cars
- construction paper
- pie plates containing liquid tempera paint

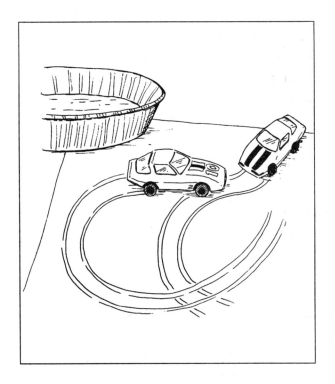

With the Child
1. Dip the wheels of one toy car lightly into paint and then "drive" them back and forth across the paper to make tracks.
2. Repeat using other vehicles for an interesting pattern.

Other Connections
- Discipleship – use with stories of following Jesus.

You have shown me the paths that lead to life. (Psalm 16:11a, Acts 2:28)

Palm Branches

On Palm Sunday, parade around the room waving these branches and shouting "Hosanna! Hurray for Jesus!"

Materials Needed
- 1 double sheet of newsprint
- tape
- scissors

With the Child
1. Tightly roll up the newsprint.
2. Tape the side of the rolled newsprint.
3. Cut long slits in the newsprint roll.
   (See illustration.)
4. Gently pull the center of the roll upwards, so that the "leaves" of the palm branch are exposed.
   (See illustration.)

Other Connections
- Creation Story
- Parable of the Mustard Seed
- Parable of the Sower

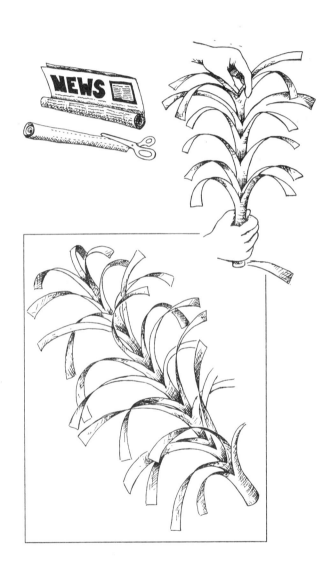

The people began to shout "Praise God! God bless him who comes in the name of the Lord!" *(Mark 11:9)*

Seed Bracelet

This is an ideal bracelet to use when taking a walk outside to look at God's creation.

Materials Needed
- masking tape
- seeds

With the Child
1. Place a piece of masking tape around the child's wrist, sticky side out, and overlap it so that it becomes a bracelet. (Note: Make it loose enough so that it moves on the wrist – however, it is not meant to come off the wrist until it is cut.)
2. Decorate the bracelet by sticking a variety of seeds to the tape.

Option
- Bend a cardboard strip into a circle and staple so that it forms a bracelet that can be removed from the wrist. Glue the strip of masking tape sticky side up around the circle, overlapping the ends so they stick together.

Other Connections
- Spring – gather tiny flowers, grass, seeds on a nature walk. Stick these to the bracelet.
- Parable of the Mustard Seed – stick small mustard seeds to the bracelet.

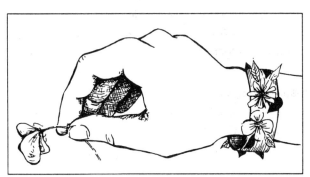

Only if a grain of wheat falls to the earth and dies will it bring forth fruit.
(John 12:24)

Yarn Cross

Very young children will need a lot of assistance to create this cross.

Materials Needed
- disposable meat tray
- long nail
- yarn
- tape
- scissors

With the Child
1. Cut meat tray in the shape of a cross.
2. Using a long nail, punch holes in the cross. *(See illustration.)*
3. Wrap a small piece of tape around the end of a length of yarn to form a "needle."
4. Push the "needle" up through a center hole.
5. Thread the yarn from the center holes out to each side, going through each hole on the sides once, and through each center hole three times.
6. Thread a shorter length of yarn through the top to form a hanger.

Other Connections
- Easter – use bright colors of yarn to create a cross for Easter Day.

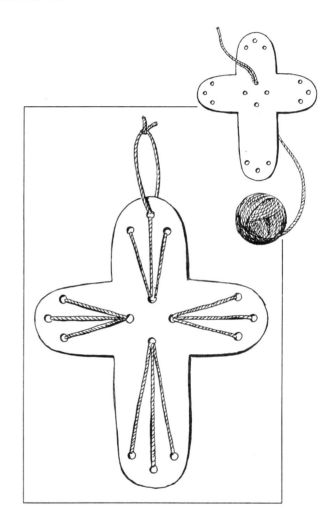

Jesus told them, "I will be put to death, but three days later I will be raised to life."　　　　　　　　　　*(Matthew 16:21b)*

Folded Paper Cross

This is fun to do and always a surprise when shown for the first time!

Materials Needed

- a sheet of letter-sized paper
- scissors

With the Child

1. Fold the piece of paper as if making a square but do not cut off the strip (Fig. 1).
2. Fold A to B (Fig. 2).
3. Fold in half (Fig. 3).
4. Fold in half again (Fig. 4).
5. Cut a straight line up the center (Fig. 5).
6. Open the paper to reveal the cross.

Other Connections

- Easter – decorate with paper flowers.

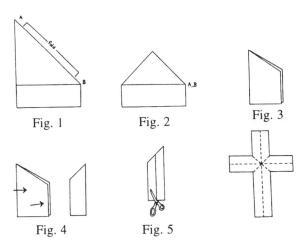

Fig. 1 Fig. 2 Fig. 3

Fig. 4 Fig. 5

For the message about Christ's death on the cross...for us who are being saved it is God's power at work. (1 Corinthians 1:18)

Flying Butterfly

These Easter butterflies actually look like they are flying!

Materials Needed

- construction paper
- a butterfly shape pattern (see p. 64)
- scissors
- drinking straw
- stapler
- crayons

With the Child

1. Use the butterfly pattern to trace a butterfly on construction paper. Cut out.
2. Decorate the butterfly with crayons. (Remember that the two wings are identical. Start a pattern on one wing and repeat it on the other wing. See suggestion below for blotting.)
3. Fold the butterfly in half. Staple along the bottom (Fig. 1).
4. Staple a straw to the base (Fig. 2). Fold back wings.
5. Move the straw up and down to make the wings of the butterfly flap.

Options

- Print "God Brings New Life" on a strip of paper and punch a hole at each end. Thread it onto the straw and let the butterfly spread the Good News!
- Decorate the butterfly by dropping paint on one side and pressing wings together to blot the paint. (Designs on both wings will be identical.)

Other Connections

- Spring
- Baptism – use a simple dove shape (see p. 62)

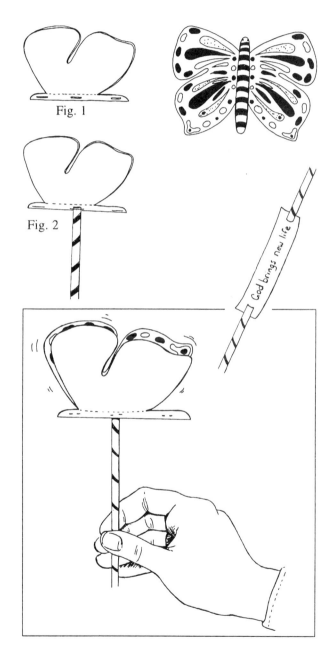

Fig. 1

Fig. 2

God brings new life

When anyone is joined to Christ, they are a new being; the old is gone, the new has come.

(2 Corinthians 5:17)

Easter Lily

The Easter lily reminds us of God's Easter promise. It even has a shape like a trumpet sounding the Good News!

Materials Needed
- white paper
- yellow construction paper
- green construction paper (optional)
- glue
- pencil
- scissors
- pipe cleaner or drinking straw
- tape
- stapler

With the Child
1. Trace child's hand on white paper and cut out.
2. Take a small piece of yellow paper (small enough to fit into the palm of the traced hand) and cut it lengthwise like grass. *(See illustration.)* Glue it to the hand.
3. Curl each paper finger around a pencil.
4. Roll the hand shape at the wrist to form a lily-shaped flower. Tape.
5. Attach flower to a drinking straw or pipe cleaner with stapler or more tape.
6. (Optional: Cut leaves from green construction paper and tape to the stem.)
7. Make several flowers and tie a ribbon around them to create a bouquet.

Other Connections
- Outreach – makes a beautiful bouquet for someone housebound.

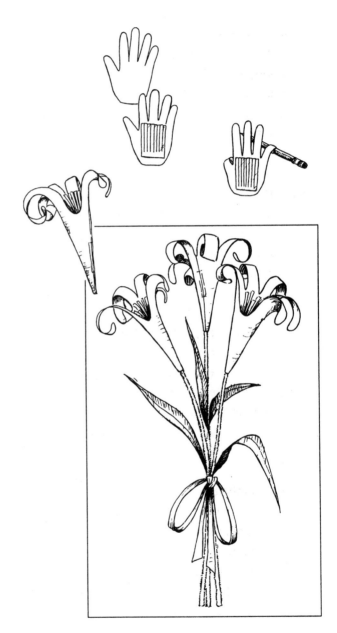

Jesus said to them, "Go throughout the whole world and preach the gospel to all people everywhere."
(Mark 16:15)

Plastic Bubble Prints

Try popping some of these bubbles and shouting "Alleluia" each time one pops!

Materials Needed
- plastic bubble packing material (used for packing fragile items)
- tempera paint and brushes
- plain paper
- masking tape
- wet cloths for cleanup

With the Child
1. Cut a large piece of package bubble wrap. Tape to a table with masking tape – bubble side up. (Resist popping these bubbles as they don't print once the bubble has been popped.)
2. Use small brushes to paint the bubbles with bright colors.
3. Lay a blank sheet of paper on the top of the painted bubbles and gently rub, making a print from the painted bubbles. Several prints can be taken before this needs to be repainted.
4. Wipe bubble wrap with a wet soapy cloth and it can be used over and over. It is not necessary to clean the crevices between each bubble.

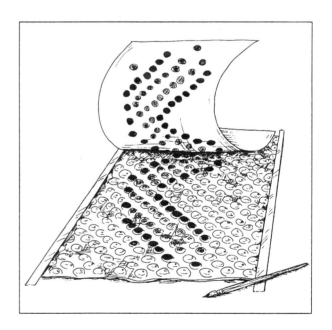

Other Connections
- Noah's Ark – use rainbow colors to make rainbow prints to remind children of God's promise.
- Celebration – use for any story that calls for a celebration. The bubbles could be popped while calling out celebratory words – just remember to use new bubble wrap for painting.

You have changed my sadness into a joyful dance.   *(Psalm 30:11a)*

Sheep Puppet

Every year during the Easter Season we encounter the passages about Jesus as The Good Shepherd.

Materials Needed
- small yogurt container or disposable cup
- white or black construction paper
- black felt pen
- white glue
- quilt batting
- scissors

With the Child
1. Cut two holes in one side of the container, large enough for a child's fingers.
2. Cut a 2 in. (5 cm) circle of white or black construction paper and draw a sheep's face on it. Glue it on the container.
3. Cut two ovals of black construction paper for the sheep's ears.
4. Glue the quilt batting on the sheep's body.
5. Add paper ears.
6. Put index and middle finger into holes to make the sheep walk.

Other Connections
- Parable of the Lost Sheep
- Reign of Christ Sunday
- Psalm 23
- Noah's Ark – use instructions to create other animals.

My sheep listen to my voice; I know them and they follow me.

(John 10:27)

Paper Cup Flowers

God's love is for everyone in the world!

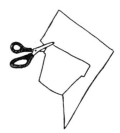

Materials Needed
- construction paper
- scissors
- felt markers or crayons
- cupcake liners
- glue sticks
- old magazines

With the Child
1. Cut a flowerpot shape and glue it onto a piece of construction paper. *(See illustration.)*
2. Draw leaves and stems coming out of the pot.
3. To form a flower, glue a cupcake liner at the top of each stem.
4. Cut out faces of people of different nationalities from catalogs and magazines and glue them in the center of each cupcake liner.

Option
- Draw a face in each cupcake liner.

Other Connections
- Christian Family Sunday
- Spring

We too are God's children.   *(Acts 17:28b)*

Circle of People

See how the Good News is spread to others!

Materials Needed

- letter-sized sheets of paper
- scissors
- crayons or felt markers
- (optional) catalogs and glue

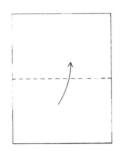

With the Child

1. Fold paper as for a snowflake. *(See illustration.)*
2. Use a pencil to draw a figure – making sure the figure touches both sides of the fold. Cut out.
3. Carefully unfold and discover all the people!
4. Draw in faces or glue faces cut from catalogs.

Option

- Mount on construction paper for stability.

Other Connections

- Stories about God's inclusive love – cut pictures of people of different ages, gender and ethnic backgrounds from catalogs.
- Pentecost
- All Saints' Day – draw pictures of people to remember.
- Christian Family Sunday – draw pictures of God's family.

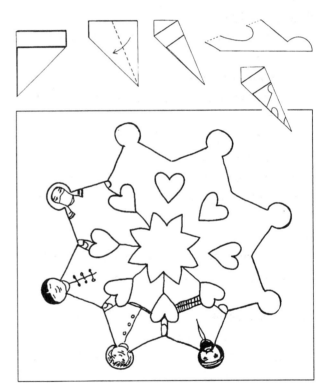

The disciples went out and preached everywhere, and the Lord worked with them and proved that their preaching was true by the miracles that were performed.
(Mark 16:20)

Ancient Scroll

Paul, and other apostles, wrote many letters to early churches to encourage them. Many of these were first written on parchment (thin leather) which was beaten or sewn together into long strips. These strips, called scrolls, were rolled up and tied together for storage.

Materials Needed
- brown paper grocery bags
- scissors
- felt markers
- yarn

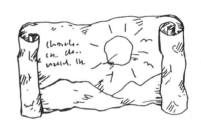

With the Children
1. Cut a large rectangular piece of paper from the grocery bag.
2. Crumple paper and smooth it out.
3. Repeat this process several times. (This will make the paper look ancient.)
4. Use felt markers to draw a picture or print a message on the paper.
5. Roll the paper from each end toward the middle and tie with yarn.

Option
- Use white paper and rub a wet tea bag over it to "antique" it. When dry, use it as scroll paper.

Other Connections
- Jesus Reads Scripture in the Temple
- Bible Verses: print particular verses worth remembering on the scrolls.
- Early Christians

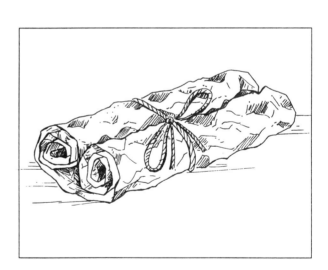

Look on our Lord's patience as the opportunity God is giving you to be saved, just as our dear brother Paul wrote to you, using the wisdom that God gave him.   *(2 Peter 3:15)*

Joyful Wind Banner

During Pentecost, parade around the room or through the church with this banner.

Materials Needed

- standard-size piece of construction paper (or small paper bag)
- scraps of paper for decoration
- crayons or felt markers
- colorful crepe paper streamers (approx. 12 x 1 in./ 30 x 1.5cm)
- tape, glue stick or stapler
- hole punch
- string
- scissors

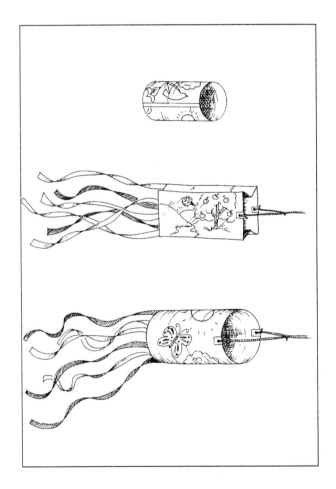

With the Child

1. Decorate the construction paper (or the small paper bag with the bottom cut off) with scraps of paper and felt markers or crayons.
2. Tape the two ends of the construction paper into a cylinder. *(See illustration.)*
3. With glue stick, tape, or stapler attach crepe paper streamers around the bottom rim.
4. Around the top rim, place two or three pieces of masking tape for reinforcement and punch a hole in each. Attach a string for holding.

Other Connections

- Spring
- Easter – decorate with an Easter message like "Alleluia!" or "He is risen!"

Suddenly there was a noise from the sky which sounded like a strong wind blowing, and it filled the whole house where they were sitting. (Acts 2:2)

Pinwheel

God's Spirit is like breath and like wind. We can't see it but we can feel its power.

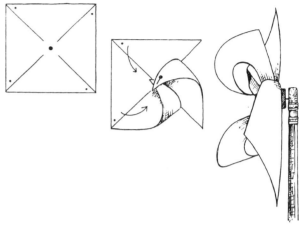

Materials Needed

- a square piece of paper
- crayons or felt markers
- scissors
- a pencil with an eraser
- a map pin
- a button

With the Child

1. Mark the center of the paper with a dot. Draw straight lines towards the center from each corner. At each corner, mark a dot on the side of each line. *(See illustration.)*
2. Color the square with Pentecost colors (i.e. orange, yellow, and red).
3. Cut along the lines towards the center.
4. Stick the pin through one dot as shown, then through each of the other points as they are turned in.
5. Then stick the pin through the dot in the center.
6. Place pencil on a flat surface.
7. Place a button behind the pinwheel (curved side toward the eraser).
8. Push pin through the button and into the eraser on the pencil.

Option

- Before the paper has been cut, use pencil crayons to draw a small picture in the corners that do not show a dot. These might be pictures of the way that God's Spirit helps us do loving, caring things.

The wind blows wherever it wishes; you hear the sound it makes, but you do not know where it comes from or where it is going. It is like that with everyone who is born of the Spirit. (John 3:8)

Flaming Hats

At Pentecost, Jesus' friends felt the wind against their faces and saw the fire dance about. Then, they ran outside to tell others about Jesus, whose stories and courage and strength filled their hearts.

Materials Needed

- 12 x 18 in. (30 x 45cm) construction paper
- scissors
- tape
- stapler
- crayons or felt markers
- red, yellow and orange tissue paper

With the Child

1. To make the cone – draw and cut out a large circle from the construction paper.
2. Cut the circle in half.
3. Decorate one of the half circles with crayons and felt markers.
4. Overlap the cut edges until the cone is sized so it fits the child's head. Staple.
5. To make the flames – cut tissue paper into large rectangles (approx. 8 x 20 in./20 x 50cm).
6. Place the three colors together and roll them into a tube. Tape to secure.
7. Cut slits in the top of the tube.
8. Gently pull the center of the tube upwards so that the flames are exposed. (Note: See Palm Branches on page 37 for a similar idea.)
9. Staple tissue paper flames to the hat.

Option

- Make a paper plate hat for the flames. Cut the center out of a paper plate and staple a paper soup bowl over the hole. Attach yarn to the side of the hat for ties.

Then they saw what looked like tongues of fire which spread out and touched each person there.   *(Acts 2:3)*

Hand Mirror

Children need to hear over and over again that God will always love them.

Materials Needed
- poster board
- scissors
- felt markers
- a small circle of mylar
- glue stick

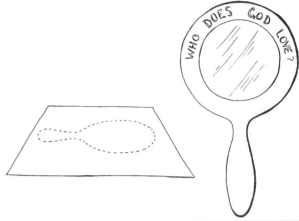

With the Child
1. Cut out a poster board mirror shape.
2. Around the edge print a phrase (e.g. "Who does God love?").
3. Glue the circle of mylar in the center of the mirror shape.
4. With felt markers decorate the front and back of the mirror around the mylar.
5. Look into the mirror and see who God loves.

Option
- Cut out a body shape and glue the mylar circle on the head. Yarn hair might be glued around the face (mylar circle) and the body could be decorated.

Other Connections
- Print other phrases on the hand mirror such as –
  "Where does God's light shine?"
  "Who is Jesus calling?"
  "Who is important to God?"

But anyone who loves God is known by God.   *(1 Corinthians 8:3)*

Creative Pillowcase

Use this pillowcase as a reminder that God is with us all through the night...and the day...and in our beginnings and in our endings, and all time in between.

Materials Needed

- a plain pillowcase
- fabric paint or fine-line permanent markers
- newspaper
- masking tape

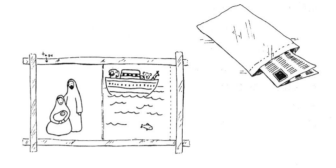

With the Child

1. Place a double sheet of newspaper inside the pillowcase (to prevent the drawing going through to the back). Smooth out the pillowcase and tape it to a table.
2. Decorate the pillowcase with the felt markers or fabric paint.
3. Print a phrase on the pillowcase (e.g. "God is always with me").
4. If using fabric paint, let this dry overnight before sleeping on it.

Other Connections

- Bible Stories – make a story pillow and illustrate a favorite Bible story on it. Or, divide the pillow in half and do two stories. (After it is dry, turn it over and draw more pictures on the other side.) Each night the child could decide where they are going to lay their head.

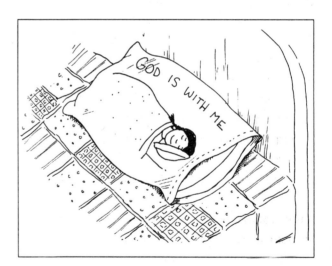

"I am the first and the last," says the Lord God Almighty, who is, who was, and who is to come.
(Revelation 1:8)

Pop-Up Puppet

Who spreads God's love? Pop up the puppet and see!

Materials Needed

- construction paper
- a disposable cup
- a dowel, drinking straw or Popsicle stick
- a fine-line pen
- tape
- yarn
- scissors
- glue

With the Child

1. Cut a 1 in. (2.5 cm) circle and "shoulder" piece from construction paper. *(See illustration.)*
2. Print child's name on the shoulders and attach it to the head.
3. Draw a face on the circle. Glue on yarn for hair.
4. Tape a drinking straw to the back of the figure.
5. Print "Who spreads God's love?" on the cup.
6. Put the straw down through the cup and have the puppet hide.
7. Read the cup and then have the puppet pop up.

Other Connections

- Samuel – print "Who did God call?" on the cup. Use this to tell the story of Samuel's call.
- Jesus and the Children – print "Who loves all the children?" on the cup. Glue a picture of Jesus, or a sticker, to the straw or Popsicle stick.
- Parable of the Lost Sheep – print "Where is the lost sheep?" on the cup. Glue a cotton ball sheep to the straw or Popsicle stick.

I will pour out my Spirit on everyone. Your sons and daughters will proclaim my message. (Acts 2:17b)

Helping Hands Booklet

Here is one way to be a faithful helper to the family.

Materials Needed
- 3 sheets of plain paper
- pencil
- scissors
- construction paper
- hole punch
- yarn
- felt markers or crayons

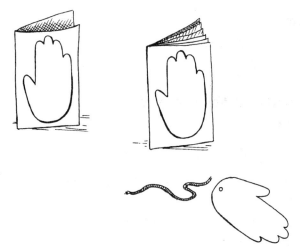

With the Child
1. Fold 3 sheets of paper in half and trace child's hand on the top sheet.
2. Cut through all sheets of paper so that there are now six hands.
3. For the cover, fold a piece of construction paper in half and trace the hand again. Cut out.
4. To make a booklet, stack the cut-out hands, beginning and ending with a construction paper hand. Punch a hole in the top, thread yarn through the hole and tie a bow. *(See illustration.)*
5. Decorate paper hands with crayons or markers.
6. Print the poem on the construction paper cover.
7. Give the booklet to someone who might like to receive this gift.

Poem
Whenever there is work to do,
Just tear out a hand
And I'll help you.

Other Connections
- Parable of the Good Samaritan

By this everyone will know that you are my disciples, if you have love for one another. (John 13:35)

Caring Bag

Use this bag to collect items for the food bank or thrift shop.

Materials Needed
- large brown paper bag
- pen or pencil
- glue
- pictures cut from magazines
- marker

With the Child
1. Trace hands several times on the outside of the bag.
2. Glue small pictures of some of the things that people need (e.g. food, clothing, medicine, friends).
3. Print a verse such as "When we help others we are helping God" on the bag with marker.
4. Fill the bag with food or clothing.

Option
- Have the child draw pictures of people they love on separate cards. Put these cards in the decorated bag. Then, at certain times, select a card and think of a way to help that person in a special way (e.g. giving a hug, playing a game with them, doing a chore to help them).

Other Connections
- Parable of the Good Samaritan

Love the Lord your God with all your heart, with all your soul, with all your mind, and with all your strength...Love your neighbor as you love yourself.
(Mark 12:30-31)

Nest Gathering

Set these bags outside so that the birds can use the contents for nest building.

Materials Needed

- a small paper bag
- bits of colorful ribbon, string, yarn
- felt markers or crayons

With the Child

1. Decorate the paper bag with colorful designs.
2. Taking the bag, go for a short walk outside and gather things that a bird might use to build a nest (e.g. twigs, leaves, grass).
3. Add bits of colorful ribbon, string or yarn from materials gathered in preparation for project.
4. Fold down the sides of the bag to form a "nest."
5. Place this gift somewhere outside for the birds to find.

Other Connections

- Creation Story
- Parable of the Good Samaritan

O Lord, how manifold are your works! In wisdom you have made them all; the earth is full of your creatures...All of them depend on you to give them food when they need it...You open your hand and they are filled with good things. *(Psalm 104:24, 27-28)*

Paper Doll

These dolls carry special messages!

Materials Needed

- 2 sheets of plain newsprint
- masking tape
- felt markers or crayons
- construction paper or a paper plate
- stapler

With the Child

1. Roll one sheet of newsprint lengthwise and then fold it in half.
2. Tape around the center with masking tape.
3. Bend the two ends out to form legs.
   (See illustration.)
4. On the second piece of newsprint, print or draw a message of things you can do well, or things you feel good about doing.
5. Roll this page widthwise with your special gifts turned to the inside.
6. Insert it through the body loop to form arms.
7. Decorate a face using a paper plate or construction paper circle.
8. Staple the face to the top of the body loop.
9. Show the dolls to others and share your hidden strengths.

Other Connections

- All Saints' Day – print names or draw pictures of people to remember before rolling up the paper.

But it is one and the same Spirit who does all this...the Spirit gives a different gift to each person.   *(1 Corinthians 12:11)*

Garbage Eater

Picking up litter is one way we can show our love for the world God created.

Materials Needed
- large brown paper bag
- construction paper scraps
- glue
- scissors
- stapler
- felt markers

With the Child
1. Cut a "mouth" opening in the lower (middle) half of the bag.
2. Fold bag flat to draw a face. Add paper hair, teeth, ears.
3. Fold top of bag over 1 in. (2.5 cm) and staple down.
4. Open bag carefully.
5. Go for a walk and feed the creature bits of litter.

Other Connections
- Creation Story
- Outreach – help a neighbor clean up their property.

The world and all that is in it belong to God; the earth and all who live in it are God's.   *(Psalm 24:1)*

Fridge Magnet

Use this magnet to hold a grace for mealtime on the refrigerator.

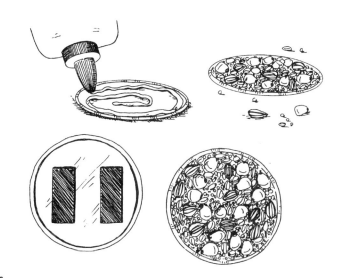

Materials Needed
- smooth juice tin lid, pill bottle lid, or bottle cap
- a variety of grains (e.g. corn, rice, oats, wheat, barley, rye)
- white glue
- magnetic strips with adhesive backing
- small squares of paper

With the Child
1. Squeeze glue in the lid or bottle cap (just enough to cover the bottom evenly).
2. Place a sampling of different grains in the lid. Cover all the spaces.
3. Peel the adhesive backing from the magnetic strips and stick these to the back of the bottle cap or lid.
4. On two or three squares of paper, print several graces to use at meal times.
5. When the magnet is dry, fasten the graces to the refrigerator with this new magnet.

Option
- Glue a photograph on the lid instead of the grains.

Other Connections
- Prayers – can also hold the picture of someone or some group who needs their prayers.
- Bible Verses – use the magnet to hold special verses.

The land has produced its harvest. God, our God, has blessed us.

(Psalm 67:6)

Table Decoration

When sharing a meal together, place this on the table as a reminder of all the things we are thankful for. This might make a nice centerpiece for Thanksgiving.

Materials Needed

- dried flowers and grasses
- a fabric circle
- play dough (see recipe on p. 61)
- thick yarn or ribbon

With the Child

1. Take a walk and gather a variety of dried flowers and grasses.
2. Place a ball of play dough in the center of a round piece of cloth fabric.
3. Insert dried flowers or grasses into the play dough.
4. Gather up the fabric around the play dough and tie with colorful ribbon or thick yarn.

Option

- Instead of fabric, place play dough into a disposable paper cup. Decorate the cup with felt markers or glue on a variety of small items (e.g. buttons, glitter, paper shapes).

Other Connections

- Outreach – give to someone who is housebound.
- Ruth and Boaz – use small stalks of grain in the play dough.

In the name of Jesus the Christ, always give thanks for everything to God.
(Ephesians 5:20)

Recipes

Coloring Cotton Balls

(for Butterfly Calendar)

- Place a small amount (e.g. 1 teaspoon (5mL) of tempera powder in a plastic bag.
- Add a supply of cotton balls, close the bag and shake.
- When cotton balls are colored, remove them and place them in another bag and shake again to remove any excess. (Note: Add more or fewer cotton balls the next time, depending on the excess.)
- Make 3 – 4 colors so that there will be a variety of colors.

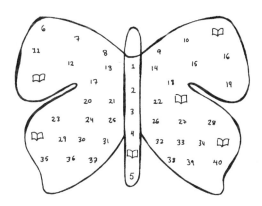

Play Dough

2 cups (500mL) flour
1 cup (250mL) water
1 cup (250 mL) salt
food coloring

Mix the flour and salt together in a large bowl. Add food coloring to the water. Slowly add mixture to the dry ingredients until ingredients are uniformly moistened. Remove dough from the bowl and knead for several minutes. Note: If using over and over again add a little cooking oil to keep it from drying out. Store in a tightly closed plastic container.

Pretzels

3 1/2 cups (875mL) flour
1 tablespoon (15mL) yeast (or one package)
1 tablespoon (15mL) sugar
1 1/3 cups (325mL) warm water, divided
1 teaspoon (5mL) salt
coarse salt

Put 1/2 cup (125mL) warm water in a warm medium size mixing bowl and stir in sugar. Sprinkle yeast on top and leave for 10 minutes. Add remaining water and salt and stir in. Stir in 2 1/2 cups (625mL) of flour with spoon then knead in last cup with hands. Turn onto a floured surface and knead till smooth. Can be shaped right away and baked.

(Note: For baking instructions, see p. 34.)

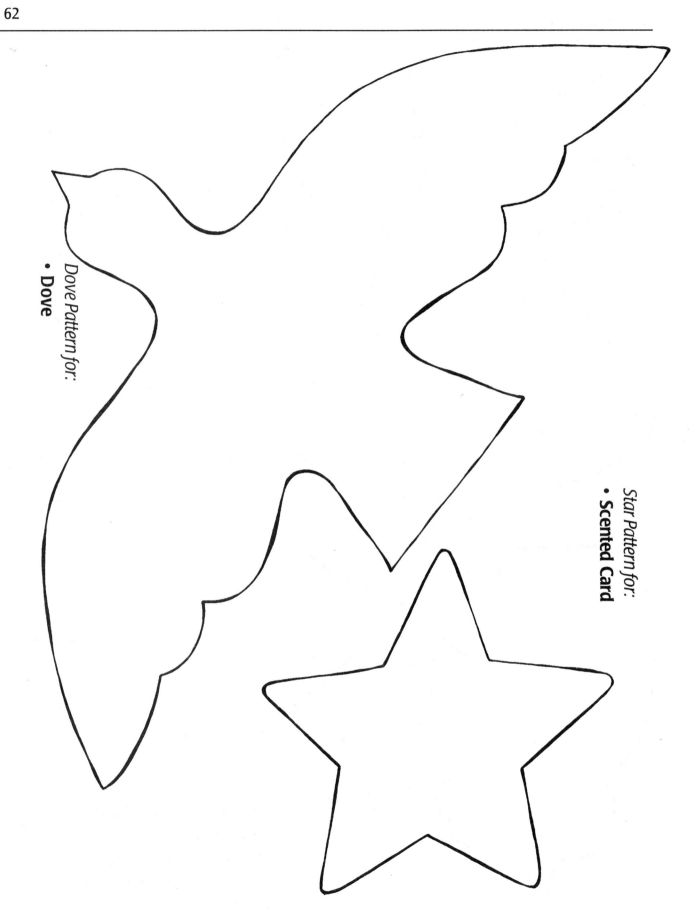

Dove Pattern for:
- **Dove**

Star Pattern for:
- **Scented Card**

Christmas Patterns for:
- **Advent Calendar Poster**
- **Scented Card**
- **Stained Glass Window**
- **Epiphany Star Streamers**

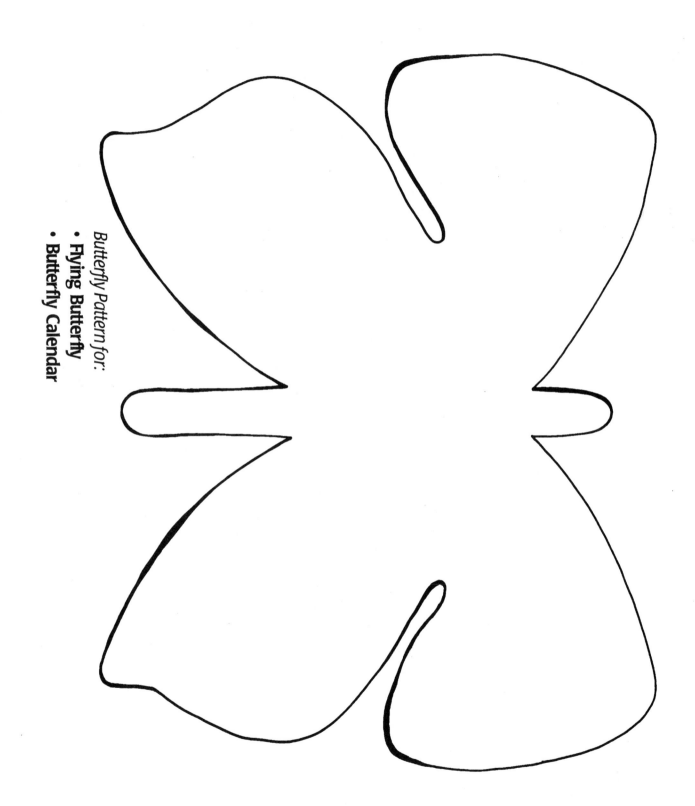

Butterfly Pattern for:
- **Flying Butterfly**
- **Butterfly Calendar**